FRISKY THE SNOWMAN

LAUREN BIEL

Library of Congress Cataloging-in-Publication Data

Frisky the Snowman/Lauren Biel 1st ed.

Cover Design: Lori Rivera

Editing: Sugar Free Editing

Interior Design: Sugar Free Editing

For more information on this book and the author, visit: www.LaurenBiel.com

Please visit LaurenBiel.com for a full list of content warnings.

This story is for my readers who fantasize about sleeping with snowmen. To the rest of you, enjoy unlocking a new kink!

AUTHOR'S NOTE

This is a spicy Christmas novelette that isn't meant to be taken too seriously. I mean, it's a story about a woman fucking a snowman! Happy Hoe-lidays!

CHAPTER ONE

Holly

$\mathcal{W}$inter rolled over my cabin in the woods like a lion overnight. In half a day, a foot of snow has fallen, rising above my feet as I stand in the doorway. Cool air whips at my legs beneath my knee-length skirt, but my ankles and feet stay warm within my winter boots. I walk into the crisp, white snow, my boots crunching and patting down the powder with every step. My gloved hand reaches down and gathers a ball of snow, packing it together before I set it down and start rolling it. The ball grows in front of me as I push it around the yard.

My thighs begin to itch from the cold, but an excited warmth keeps me going. I've waited for this first real snow-fall for weeks, and no amount of cold will stop me from what I've planned. I rub the snowball's large curves and twitch with anticipation. A soft sigh escapes me. Nothing is as perfectly wonderful as a round ball of pure white.

Once the first ball is too large to fit my arms around, I start working on the next. Breath seeps out of me in visible clouds. My nipples harden to painful points as the cold sinks below my clothes. But I don't care. I keep going until I roll the second ball beside the first.

Before I put it where it belongs, I stop to straddle the first mound of snow. The hard-packed ice freezes my slit as I rub it along the friction-filled surface.

There's something about snow for me. I'm obsessed with the stuff. Most people find building a snowman fun, but I find it *erotic*. I'm crafting a perfect man, with a big, round lower body, a smooth midriff, and a perfectly shaped "head" on top.

With a grunt, I raise the second ball and place it on the first. Now I can begin to work on the head—my favorite part.

I roll and shape and roll some more until I'm happy with the size. My snowman must be proportional, after all, and he needs enough space for his handsome features. I plop this final ball on top of the first two and rush inside to grab his other necessities.

The backpack I packed an hour ago sits by the entryway. It rattles a bit as I hoist it over my shoulder and head back outside. I drop it beside my snowy hunk and dig around in the bag's open mouth. Pieces of coal rattle in my hand as I stare at the three-piece man in front of me. I stick one black orb into the left side of his face, then another into the right. They're a bit lopsided, and that just won't do. I adjust them until they're even. Snow is forgiving that way.

Using a few more pieces of coal, I form his mouth into a cute and permanent smile, leaving a vacant space just above it for his nose. As I step back to survey my work so far, my foot bumps the backpack and sends the contents tumbling out. I grip one of the carrots and put it in place.

"Your nose, sir," I say through a laugh as I pack a little snow around it to keep it in place.

My gaze drops to the bag once more, and I spot the pièce de résistance—the biggest carrot I could find at the store. Like, scary big. I wrap my hands around it and smile.

"But he already has a nose," I whisper, tapping the carrot across my chest. "What could he possibly need another one of these for?"

My eyes drop to the huge, round, sexy ball at the bottom of his body, and I shove the carrot's base into the packed snow. My grunts punctuate the night air as I struggle to get it in, but the snow finally spreads enough to let me attach his glorious accent piece.

I step back and stare at the man I created. My big, white snowman with a nice-sized carrot dick.

"I dub thee Frisky the snowman," I say, putting my hands on my hips.

I bunch my skirt around my waist and expose my naked ass to the cold air, then I step into him and run my warm tongue along his mouth. A gritty mixture of coal and snow brushes over my lips. As I kiss him, I reach down and stroke his carrot. The ungodly large vegetable fills my entire palm. The warm wetness between my legs intensifies as I stroke and kiss him until I'm almost ready to burst. If he were human, I'm sure he would have by now.

My hands race over what would be his shoulders, and I lean back. "Whoops! I almost forgot your arms."

I grab the sticks from the pile next to him and stab one into each side of his midriff. He's nearly perfect now. I consider using a few more pieces of coal for buttons, but I decide against it. I can dress him later if I wish . . . once I've had some fun.

I pull off my gloves and drop them into the snow. My zipper squeaks as I pull it down and spread my jacket. When

I lower my cami, my breasts fall from the fabric. I rub the edge of his forked stick arm along my pebbling skin.

"Do you like how my tits feel, Frisky?" I moan. "Do you want me to fuck you? Do you want me to ride your long, hard, orange cock?" I turn and back myself against the big snowy ball. The carrot fills my hand as I ease myself onto it, and I gasp as Frisky fills the aching space between my thighs.

It's been nearly a year since I've felt this good. I fuck myself with carrots the other nine months out of the year, but it's not the same. I've tried. Nothing compares to the firm body of an icy snowman. I even filled pillowcases with ice one summer to see if I could replicate the feeling, but nothing comes close to this.

"Fuck, you feel so good," I pant. I lean back so I can feel him behind me. His cold body is like a wall. God, it's electric, even as my thighs become numb.

The ice begins to burn the hand I've wrapped around the carrot, but I can't stop. I dip my other hand between my legs and rub my clit. In theory, it should be hard to come with both the skin of my clit and fingers so frozen, but I can almost mentally get off from knowing the security camera is catching everything.

I'll be able to fuck myself to me fucking Frisky all year long.

I look up at the camera and smirk before throwing my head back as the explosion of warm come washes between my legs. I orgasm hard enough to rip off his big carrot cock. It sinks into the snow between my feet. I kneel and wrap my lips around the carrot, holding it between my teeth, then I place it back in the original location. The correct position.

I grip the base and wiggle it back in, but before I let go, I suck more of the orange member into my mouth until my nose is nearly touching the snow. Cold air mixes with my warm breath, but I won't stop until I've cleaned my come from his cock.

When I've finished my task, I lean back on my heels to give my knees a break from the frigid ground. My gaze dashes around the dark backyard. I contemplate hiding his cock, because it's mine, but I leave it attached. Though I know no one else will see him on this back road, it still excites me to know that *if* someone drove down this road, they'd see the used carrot sticking out of his lap. My carrot. The one I buried deep in my pussy.

I get to my feet and place a kiss on his frozen cheek. "See you tomorrow, Frisky."

CHAPTER TWO

Frisky

'm immovable but not emotionless. I think and feel. My first memory is of that woman's tongue along my mouth, then the warmth of her plump breast against my hand. I tried to move, to rock with her motions and feel more of her soft skin, but I couldn't. As I try again now, my fingers refuse to wiggle unless a strong breeze moves them for me. I can only look directly ahead, at a dark forest and a mailbox. I try to speak, but my lips remain in place.

What happened? What am I? And where did the beautiful woman go?

I want to feel what I felt when she was in front of me. I didn't know what was happening, but the wet warmth, the tightness . . . I need more. I have no choice but to sit and wait for her to appear again. I'm at her mercy.

The sun goes down, sending blinding rays of light against

the snow. The night sky glows with stars. A gentle creaking sound interrupts the silent night, and footsteps approach. I want to turn my head and glimpse her again, because I know she's behind me. Warmth radiates from her body, and the familiar scent of cinnamon grows stronger. When she finally appears in front of me, a warm tingle rushes toward my lower body.

Her beautiful blonde hair sits in a sloppy bun on her head, and purple earmuffs cover her ears. A pink hue tints her nose and cheeks. She's wearing a skirt again, though this one is a bit shorter. It reveals the tops of her thighs, and I long to grip them. A hint of torture taints the pleasure she brings me, but I don't care. I just want to feel her again.

"Evening, Frisky," she whispers before running her tongue along my lips again.

Hello, snow princess, I want to say, but my mouth doesn't cooperate. The soft pad of her tongue rolls over each piece of coal. *Lower with that mouth,* I whisper in my head.

As if she somehow hears me, she drops to her bare knees, rips off a glove, and wraps a warm hand around something on my lower body. "Have you been waiting for me to come out and touch your cock?" she whispers.

Yes, fucking touch my cock.

I'm guessing my cock is right where that warm tingle happened. And it's happening again as her fingers stroke me. The sensation shifts, and now wet warmth engulfs me. It's similar to what I felt when she kissed my coal lips, so I assume she's using her mouth on me. I can't look down and see her, but I feel each hungry bob of her head and envision what that must look like.

Fucking perfection.

She sucks on me until I'm certain her knees are ice, and then she stands and eyes me with a dark hunger as she raises her little skirt and straddles me. The warmth between her legs is like a furnace compared to the cold I'm made of.

"Do you want to be inside me, Frisky?" It sounds like a question, but I realize it's not as she rubs her slit against me. She'll fuck me regardless of my wishes. Lucky for me, we both want the same thing.

Her arms wrap around me as she lowers herself on me, and every part she touches becomes sentient. When her pussy wraps around me, when it clenches and grips me, I'm done for.

She buries me deep, and I wish I could fuck her in the way she deserves. I long to pull her against me before I rail her. But experiencing this is a gift, even if I can't actively participate.

She grips me as she rides me, fucking me until my cock pops off. I can no longer feel her wrapped around me when it disengages from my body, which is a shame. I want to know what she feels like when she comes. She's a fucking angel, and I've never seen anyone so beautiful and perfect.

Her feral screams quiet and her body stops quivering. With a pleasure-filled sigh, she leans against me.

Good girl, snow princess.

She pulls the carrot from inside her, cleans it off with her mouth, and reattaches it before standing and turning to face me. "I forgot to give you a hat," she whispers. She eases a beanie from her coat pocket and plops it onto my head. The fabric doesn't fit around my head, but it stays in place. "See you soon, Frisky." She places a final kiss on my lips and goes inside.

I MUST HAVE FALLEN ASLEEP, because I wake up confused as shit. I take a step back and nearly scream because I *took a fucking step back*. I wiggle my fingers and look down when they move. I'm no longer made of snow. And I'm naked. Jesus. I rush to the window and stare at my reflection with a dropped jaw.

I look like her.

Like a human.

I touch my face before looking back at the spot I came from. Footprints pepper the snow, but there's no sign of my previous existence. "Snow princess," I whisper, and the sound of my own voice startles me.

I want to see her. She created me, after all. I follow her cinnamon scent to the front door and try the knob. It turns in my grasp, so I push open the door and step into a rush of warm air. Much warmer than I'm used to.

Shit, I'm going to melt!

Panic seizes me, especially when a drop of liquid falls from my forehead. I'll have to act quickly.

I follow her scent through the dark hallway until it grows stronger, and I stop in front of a door. Her bedroom, I'm guessing. With a gentle push, the door eases open and I sneak inside the room. Her scent overpowers me here. It's intoxicating.

My eyes adjust to the darkness, and I spot her sleeping form on the bed. I creep closer. The gentle curves of her cleavage rise and fall with each even breath she takes. Her perfectly pouted lips call to me, but I don't want to wake her.

A flash of light and movement catches my eyes, and I look closer. In her hand rests her phone. A video plays on a loop. I recognize what's happening on the screen because I was there, but I looked much different.

Panic ratchets through me again.

She was attracted to the me I was before, so what will she

think when she sees me like this? I'm no longer white and cold and motionless. My round curves and stick arms have been replaced by skin and warmth. She won't want *this*.

I glance down at my cock. It's still very large, orange, and thick all the way to the tip. I grip it and tug. Unlike before, it doesn't pop off. This is a slight improvement, but is it enough?

She shifts in the bed, and her breasts pop from the top of her thin shirt. Hunger rushes through me at the sight of her perfection. I want to suck, taste, and touch. But I can't. She can never know what I am.

I pick up her phone and delete the clips of me running into the house as a human, then I disarm the cameras. That takes care of one problem, but it does nothing for the ache I feel inside. Maybe if I touch myself the way she touched me, I can ease this discomfort.

I lie beside her in the bed and wrap my hand around my cock. I imagine her fucking me. I imagine me fucking her. The warm tingle grows and spreads, and come shoots from my cock and lands beside her on the bed. A heady peppermint aroma overpowers her cinnamon scent. She's sure to wake up now.

I ease out of the bed and rush from the house. Once I'm back in my spot, I rip the hat from my head. It's causing me to melt faster, and I can't have that. I want to see her again. I can only hope that I'll return to my snowy form by morning. She can't ever see me like this.

"See you soon, snow princess," I whisper.

CHAPTER THREE

Holly

I sigh and transfer my sheets from the washer to the dryer. I don't know what wetness I woke up in, but it was all over my sheets. It smelled like peppermint candy and was sort of sticky as well, but the wash seems to have removed the sweet smell. I had a shit day at work, and cleaning my sheets was the last thing I wanted to do.

I go to the window and stare at Frisky. He could relieve my tension, but I prefer to wait until night for our . . . activities. Something dark moves in the breeze, and I realize his hat has blown onto his stick hand. Wrapping my coat around me, I hurry outside and place it back on his head.

"Wouldn't want you to catch a cold," I say with a giggle.

My gaze drifts lower. So tempting.

I hurry back inside, go to the fridge, and pull a carrot from the drawer. After washing it, I lower my pants and prop myself on the kitchen island. My legs spread and I begin teasing myself with the cold vegetable. It isn't as thick as Frisky's carrot cock, but it will get the job done.

If anyone happens by the kitchen windows in front of and behind me, they'll get a real show, but I don't care. There are perks to living in the middle of nowhere, such as the ability to fuck myself in a big room full of windows. The risk only adds to my excitement.

A gasp leaves my mouth as I push the carrot past my entrance. My hand works at a feverish pace to thrust it against the place inside me that makes my toes curl. I close my eyes and imagine I'm with Frisky. He has hands that touch me in all the right places, and he pounds into me as he fucks me senseless.

My thighs quiver, and I throw my head back as the familiar tightening engulfs the space between my legs. I yank out the carrot just in time to gush all over the kitchen floor. Thank god for linoleum. Easy cleanup. I bathe in the after-shocks of my orgasm until I'm satisfied, then I mop up the mess I made and toss the carrot into the trash.

The wind has picked up outside, sending an eerie whistle through the eaves. Something clatters across my porch, startling me. I find my pants, put them on, and head outside.

Darkness blankets my property, but in the glow of the floodlights I see that some of my heavy clay decor has fallen over. Terra cotta remains litter the porch boards, but I'll have to sweep them up later. I have plans tonight.

As I turn to go inside, something catches my eye. Rather, the *absence* of something catches my eye.

Frisky no longer stands on my front lawn.

I cram my feet into my boots and rush to the spot where he once stood. I expect to see some sign of him—clumps of snow, his hat and eyes—but he's just gone. Footprints mark the snow, but they're too large to be mine. The hair on the back of my neck stands on end as I follow their path.

Someone was outside my cabin.

The wind continues to whip against me as I wrap my arms around my shivering body. The footsteps lead around the corner of the house, but I stop before I round the edge. What if this person is back there . . . waiting for me? I need some kind of weapon.

On tiptoes, I creep back to the front of the house and grab a shovel resting beside the porch. I silently thank myself for not putting it back in the shed after I planted bushes in the spring. Sometimes it pays to be forgetful. Or lazy.

With numb fingers wrapped around the wooden handle, I make my way toward the back of the house. The floodlights cast a long shadow across the snow, stretching just far enough that I can see it without peering past the corner of the building. This helps me determine exactly where this person stands, which is right in front of my kitchen window. Whoever they are, they had a front-row seat to the show I just put on. Heat rushes into my cheeks.

I take a deep breath, raise the shovel, and rush around the side of the cabin. My brain can't process what I see.

Frisky stands in front of the kitchen window, his branch hand down by his carrot cock. He looks as if he's masturbating, but that's not possible. He's a fucking snowman. Which means . . .

Someone knows what I've been doing with him and moved him over to the window as a joke.

My cheeks flame hot now, and I feel like I've been sitting in front of a fireplace instead of out in the snow with a shovel in my hands. Questions spring into my mind. How did they move him so quickly? Hell, how did they move him *at all*? He must weigh at least two hundred pounds. I packed him well . . . for reasons.

There's no way I can move him—the ice has frozen his sections together—so I guess I have a masturbating snowman as a backyard decoration now. And a creepy stalker. I peer through the darkness surrounding my property. They could be watching me right now.

A shiver runs through me, and I nearly scream when something bumps against my boot. I look down at something dark in the snow. Frisky's hat has blown off again. With a frustrated groan, I plop his hat on his head. I'm not in the mood to play with him anymore tonight. He's not in line with my camera overlooking the front yard anyway. What a mess.

"Not tonight, Frisky," I whisper, wrapping my arms around him. None of this is his fault, after all.

I hope the jerks enjoyed my show, because they won't get another one. The risk of being seen is one thing, but having someone watch you and play mean pranks is another. And what about poor Frisky?

I check him over to be sure they didn't damage him, but I find nothing out of place. While the rational part of my brain knows he's just an inanimate object made of snow, coal, and carrots, I find myself oddly attached to him. The thought of someone hurting him cinches a chain around my heart.

The cameras!

I pull my phone from my pocket and flick to the app, but my stomach sinks. Nothing has been recorded for twenty-four hours, meaning the stalker found a way to hack into my system. I arm them again.

With one last look into the woods, I hurry back into my house. I have a date tonight, and while I don't feel flirty right now, maybe getting out for a bit is exactly what I need.

CHAPTER FOUR

Frisky

I nearly got caught. I'd been watching her as she fucked herself with the same thing that made up my nose. I wanted to be what was in her hand, to fuck her like that, but the wind blew out of nowhere and took my hat with it. I became a snowman again before I could finish, and then she came outside and seemed really upset.

When she'd placed my hat on my head again, I'd wanted to show myself to her. I've gained some control of the transformations. When I'm wearing the hat, I can become human at will. When it comes off, I'm back to being a frozen snowman. But I can't risk showing myself to her and losing her forever.

I can't exist without her.

She occupies every thought, fills every conscious moment I've ever known. I have to see her. I need to get inside her house.

I can't get my hands on her phone to disarm the cameras again, so I try back windows until one gives way. I climb inside and bathe in her cinnamon scent. *Focus*, I remind myself. I just need to find her and see her, and then I can go back outside.

I creep through the house in search of her. Through parted curtains, I realize her car isn't in the driveway. She's not here.

I clutch my chest. It physically pains me to be away from her. I want to walk down the street and search for her, but there's no place in the world for a monstrosity like me.

So I wait.

I sit on the couch, breathing in her warm musk. When her scent overpowers me, I whip out my cock and start stroking myself. My head drops back as I imagine her riding my lap. Her human flesh against mine. The way she'd bounce on me and push her perfect tits into my face. My hand strokes harder and faster until a peppermint-scented load shoots from my cock.

Well, shit. I need to get better control of that.

Tires roll over the packed snow, and panic seizes my lungs. I rush to the window and spot my snow princess turning into the driveway with a man in the passenger seat. I don't have time to clean up the mess I made on her couch, so I book it out the window and face the house once more.

I struggle to transform into the snowman she loves. It's easier to shift the other way—from snowman to man. If I take off the hat, the change would be almost instantaneous, but then I can't move outside the windows and watch how things progress between them.

I take a deep breath and imagine myself as the snowman. My feet become one with the cold and within the blink of my eyes, I'm immoveable again. The reflection staring back at me is that of the snowman.

The front door opens, and they come through the house together, arm in arm.

"Chad, do you want a drink?" she asks the man.

He nods and she stumbles toward the fridge. She's been drinking already, it seems.

Her gaze lingers on the vegetable drawer, and I know she's thinking about me. Well, the carrots attached to me. The man steps into her, rubbing himself against her. She laughs as she rights herself and turns to hand him a beer. When he kisses her, white-hot jealousy burns in my frozen belly.

With a playful smile, she tries to ease away from the man, but he won't give up. He tries again, his hands wandering further.

"No!" she says, more firmly this time.

His hands paw at her, and fear twists her face. My beautiful snow princess. I can't let him hurt her. I shift into my human form, run to the front door, and make my way through the kitchen. She says no over and over now, and I hear tearing cloth as I round the corner. I rush toward them, wrapping my arm around Chad's throat.

What a stupid fucking name.

"Hey, man!" he yells. "What the fuck?"

My snow princess screams and backs away from both of us. I drag the kicking and screaming man outside, tightening my grip as we reach the doorway. His legs continue to flail against me, but he makes no sound now.

"When a woman says no, you listen," I snarl through gritted teeth.

I drag him toward the woods as he claws and digs at my wrists. Let him fight all he wants. I'm a fucking snowman. With a flick of my hat, I'll be snow again. But not before I ensure that the snow princess will be safe.

It takes so little out of me to squeeze just a bit harder,

cutting off his airway completely. His face reddens and nearly goes purple—a stark contrast against the pure snow. Something in his throat crunches, and red liquid bubbles from his mouth. Once I'm sure he's dead, I drop him in the snow.

His flaccid cock falls from his unzipped jeans, and a sudden insecurity overwhelms me. It looks nothing like what I have between my legs. The same peachy tone as his skin covers the stubby length, and it's not nearly as thick or long as mine. And it's certainly not orange. What if my snow princess doesn't want what I have to offer her?

I look down at the body again. I'll have to deal with it later.

For now, I need to check on my snow princess.

I run back toward the house. My bare feet redden in the snow, but I'm used to the cold. It doesn't actually hurt me. That's why I can stay naked outside without getting frostbitten. I was born from the snow.

I burst through the front door, but my snow princess is no longer in the kitchen. I don't want to greet her while I'm still naked, so I return to the closet in the hall. When I was searching for her earlier, I saw some men's clothing there. There isn't much to choose from, but I squeeze into a flannel shirt and some jeans, then I walk toward her bedroom.

"Get out! I'm calling the police!" she screams as I open the door.

I race across the room and grab her, and she flails against me as I wrap my arms around her and inhale her scent. God, she smells incredible.

"Get off me!" she screams. This frustrated cry makes my heart ache. I don't want to upset my snow princess, but I can't allow her to call the police. I just need some time to explain things to her and show her who I am.

She throws her body back, but I don't release her. I carry

her to the bed and pin her down, then I grab the phone and smash it against the wall. She whimpers as I pin her arms.

Touching her like this overwhelms me. My body burns for her, and I can hardly handle the heat. I need her to listen before I start to melt.

"Snow princess," I whisper. "I don't want to hurt you!"

"Then let me go!"

"I can't. You don't understand."

Her dark eyes rise to mine. "Try me."

She won't understand. She won't believe me if I try to explain. I need time to think, so I rip down her stockings as fear blitzes her face. Instead of doing anything else to her, I wrap her wrists with the fabric and tie her to the bed. I have to figure out what to do, and I can't think straight when her skin touches mine.

"Please." Her screams turn to a whimper. "Don't hurt me."

"I *really* don't want to, snow princess," I say.

"Stop calling me that!"

"You haven't told me your name."

"Holly," she whispers.

I smirk and touch her face. "I like snow princess better."

As I leave the room to find the thermostat before I burn out of my skin, she asks my name. I don't answer her. My name doesn't work as well in my human form.

She takes up screaming again as I search for the thermostat. I find it in the living room and turn the dial as low as it can go, which is only to fifty. It's still warmer than I'd like, but it's better than seventy-two. I tug at the flannel's collar before stripping off the shirt completely. I press my bare back against the cool kitchen window.

What will I do with my little snow princess now?

CHAPTER FIVE

Holly

*W*hat the fuck is happening? A man getting too forceful isn't an uncommon thing—men like Chad are a dime a dozen, and it serves me right for going out with a man named fucking Chad—but getting "rescued" by a naked mystery man doesn't exactly happen on a daily basis. I rattle my wrists against the restraints. Can I really consider myself "rescued" when I'm tied to the bed?

My throat burns from screaming, and I'm forced to rest my voice. There's no point in crying for help, anyway. I live in the middle of Bumfuck Nowhere.

Footsteps approach the bedroom, and I brace myself as the door swings open. He takes up the entire door frame. An artistic statue of male perfection. And he's fucking shirtless. I peer at the bulging area in the crotch of his jeans and wish I could have caught a glimpse of *that*, but he'd been behind Chad when he was naked.

"Snow princess," he whispers, and his eyes light up when he sees me.

"Why do you call me that?" I ask.

"Because you love the snow, princess." Infatuation saturates each word, and he eyes me like he knows what I look like without any clothes on.

Is he the man who's been watching me?

Heat fills my cheeks. How long has he been spying on me and witnessing my depraved acts with innocent little snowmen? I always said I didn't care who happened by and saw my indiscretions, but now that I'm confronted with someone who actually has, I'd consider myself a fucking liar.

I'm horrified. How desperate did I fucking look? If a hole could open in the floor and swallow me alive, I'd go without so much as a whimper.

I can get dick. I almost got Chad's dick, whether I wanted it or not! I just like the cold feeling of snow and the dirty taboo nature of fucking myself with vegetables instead of cock-shaped toys. Or real men. Is that really such a bad thing?

I lick my lips and clear my throat, trying to regain some composure. "You've been watching me?"

"Every moment I could."

He admits this so brazenly that I almost laugh. He doesn't even try to pretend he hasn't been a creep. But why would a dude who looks like him need to stalk and tie up a woman? With that body and his ice-blue eyes and blond hair, he could get a woman tied up just fine without the rest of the shit.

"What do you want with me? Are you going to hurt me?"

Surprise widens his eyes as he shakes his head and steps closer. His lips spread, and his eyebrows furrow. "I would never hurt you. You're my snow princess. My reason for breathing. My only desire is to please you."

Please me? What the fuck kind of abduction is this? I

mean, if he wants to give me an endless barrage of orgasms, he doesn't need to tie me up to accomplish his goal.

"You want to please me, huh? And what do you get out of it?"

"My pleasure is directly linked to yours," he says. "If I make you feel good, I feel good."

"Show me," I whisper, taking the risk. If he wants to please me, go nuts, dude.

If he wants to give me mind-bending orgasms, who am I to stop him? Not that I could, even if I wanted to. He could overpower me with the muscles in his pointer finger.

A smile spreads on his face, and he approaches the bed. I draw in a breath when his powerful body pushes between my legs. My thighs part. His chest presses against mine. He leans over and releases a warm breath against my ear. Goose-bumps speckle my skin, followed by a shiver of undeniable need through my body.

He leans back and surveys me before his hands grip the collar of my flimsy dress. In one seamless movement, he tears the fabric down the middle. I'm not wearing a bra, so his eyes travel straight to my bare breasts. A low growl rumbles from his chest.

"You're so perfect," he whispers.

As I lie here with my nipples pointing to the ceiling and begging for his mouth, he gets off the bed and leaves the room. A few seconds later, the front door slams and a thousand thoughts rush through my mind.

Was this all some sick game? Does he plan to murder me now, or will he just leave me to be found like this? I wiggle my wrists against the restraints, but it's no use. There's too little give. Damn these industrial-strength stockings.

I'm three seconds from dislocating my thumbs when he enters the room again. Instead of a weapon, he holds a tightly packed ball of snow in his massive hand.

"What do you plan to do with that?" I ask.

Instead of answering me, he steps toward the bed and runs the snowball down the curve of my left breast. My nipple tightens to the point of discomfort, yet I revel in this feeling. Rubbing snow against my bare body is one thing, but to have someone embrace my kink and do it for me is something else entirely.

He drags the ball of ice over my nipple in tight circles. "You love the cold, but what about the heat that follows?"

Before I can ask what he means, his hot mouth engulfs the aching nub. My back rises from the mattress, pushing my breast against him as he sucks and teases me. As he continues to devour me, he traces a path on my skin with the snowball. A cold, wet trail travels from my sternum to the curve of my stomach.

His lips move to the path left in the snow's wake, and his tongue lashes at the icy liquid. By the time he reaches my stomach, I'm tilting my pelvis to encourage him to keep going. I writhe against the restraints, which just makes me feel helpless.

At his mercy.

And I've never been so turned on.

He sits up and works the snow between his hands until it shifts from a ball to a cylinder. He presses the icy tip to my leg, running it up one thigh and down the other, then he holds it against my panties. I've never wanted something to touch me more.

"Please," I beg.

"Please what?" He moves the frozen rod away from me. "You want to feel the cold on your pretty little pussy?"

I nod with embarrassing enthusiasm.

I expect him to pull my panties aside and tease me some more, but he holds the snow cylinder between his full lips and hooks his hands into my waistband. In one swift motion, he rips the lacy material from my body and clasps his hand around the snowy rod again. He slides the cold cylinder between my lips, and my clit screams from the sudden intense shift in temperature. The cold eases away from my skin, and his warm breath replaces it. After another breath, his tongue is on me. My hips buck against each drawn-out lick as pleasure rushes between my legs. His warmth chases away the cold—one intense sensation traded for another.

He pushes the packed snow inside me, and I strain against the restraints as my back arches. He fucks me with the snow, plunging the stiff cold into me as his tongue flicks my clit. Breath shudders out of me as each pass of his mouth works in time with each forward thrust of his hand. My body quivers, and an explosion of melted snow erupts from me as I come.

Even as my orgasm wanes, he continues thrusting the melting rod. He continues licking me. He continues pleasing me until I come again. Stars dance behind my clenched eyelids, and I can't hold back the cry of pleasure that claws up my throat.

And he still doesn't stop.

Once the heat of my pussy melts the rest of the snow, his fingers replace it and piston through the soaked mess between my legs. He moans, and the deep sound vibrates against my clit. It's as if he can feel the same pleasure he's giving me.

Speaking of his pleasure, I want to feel him inside me. I want to know how that massive bulge in his pants will fit into the intimate space between my legs. His fingers are great, but I want him to fill me with his cock.

"Fuck me," I whisper.

"I can't," he says as he stops licking me and climbs up my body.

His rock-hard erection presses through his jeans against my pelvis. "It sure feels like you could."

"It's not about me, snow princess," he whispers. He pulls the ties on my restraints and releases my arms. "Besides . . . I'm not finished with you yet."

CHAPTER SIX

Frisky

I drag her out of the bedroom, and she strips away the ripped fabric as we walk toward the kitchen. I grip her waist and lift her onto the island countertop, then I step back, keeping my eyes on her as I reach into the fridge and pull the largest carrot I can find from the vegetable drawer. Her eyes fixate on the orange vegetable, and an adorable smile creeps across her face.

"Before you fuck me with that," she says, "you need to tell me your name."

"You can call me 'F.' And I want you to fuck *yourself* with this. Just like I watched you do in this kitchen."

I place the carrot into her hand. She studies it for a moment before spreading her thighs and leaning back. With her eyes trained on me, she pushes the carrot inside her. It's the most beautiful sight I've ever seen, and the best part?

Just like outside the window, I can feel what that fucking vegetable feels.

Warmth squeezes my shaft, and I grip the countertop as I try to keep control of the pleasure in my jeans. I'd hate to come in my pants at the sight alone, but pleasure overwhelms me each time I see that carrot disappear inside her.

Slick coats her swollen clit. I need to taste her.

I grab a napkin and step into her, unable to hold back any longer. With her gleaming clit laid out in front of me and her lips spread around the vegetable, I'm only torturing myself. I lean closer and lap up the wetness. She cries out, making the most beautiful sounds I've ever heard as I lift her leg and bury my face in her pussy.

I unbutton my jeans and unzip them so I can slip my hand into my pants. I stroke myself, keeping my cock hidden from her as her pussy squeezes the carrot and the feeling tightens around my cock. I growl against her clit, the vibrations strangling more moans out of her.

"I'm coming," she whimpers.

"Me too," I growl. My come spurts into the napkin.

Her panting breaths recede, and her back drops to the counter. She tilts her head to look at my cock, but I raise the fabric before she can. I ball up the napkin and toss it into the garbage before she can catch a whiff of the shameful peppermint perfume.

"Please fuck me," she whispers, her voice hoarse.

I wish I could. I'd love nothing more than to feel her around me. But I can't. I can only come to her pleasure, and I don't want her to be disgusted by the monstrosity between my legs.

"I can't."

She crawls off the counter and her wet, naked body presses against mine. She reaches for my zipper, but I grab her wrist and tug it away.

"Why?" she demands.

"You would never believe me."

"Try me!"

I take a deep breath. "I'm in love with you. You're everything to me . . . because you made me."

She cocks her head, and her eyebrows pull together. "What?"

"I'm the snowman."

She laughs, clutching her belly as the musical sound rolls from her depths. "Yeah, okay," she says when she catches her breath.

"Go look outside."

She walks to the kitchen window, cups her hands around her eyes, and peers outside. The snowman—me—is nowhere to be found.

"Clearly you moved him," she says.

"Don't you recognize the hat?"

She turns and studies the beanie on my head. "You probably took it off him. So not only are you a stalker, you're a thief," she says with snarky sarcasm. "Listen, I don't care who you are or why you're here, but you can't do everything you did to me and not have sex with me. Tease."

How the hell can I prove it to her? Do I have to turn into a fucking snowman in front of her?

She'll probably like that, actually.

"I'll prove it to you," I say as I try to turn myself into the snowman she loves.

But I can't do it.

My feet press against linoleum, not snow. The house lacks the frosty air I feel against my skin outside. No matter how I try to push these thoughts away, I'm not in the right environment for the change. My body realizes I'll melt too quickly if I transform in this space.

I grip the hat. Removing it now comes with so many

risks. When I'm a snowman again, I'll start melting, and without the hat, I can't change back unless she puts it on my head. And she may not. This could all end right now.

No more pleasing her.

I'd still feel the pleasure she brings herself, but that's not enough for me anymore. And it can only last until I melt. Even if I make the change outside, I'll eventually become water, then ice as the ground freezes. I'll be gone forever. But that's better than living without her.

I rip the hat from my head, and it falls to the ground.

Within several blinks, I become the snowman again. Her perfect tits sit in front of my eyes, but I wish I could have seen her expression when I changed. She steps back, and I can see the snarky smile on her face.

"Holy shit," she breathes.

She eyes me up and down before wrapping her arms around me. Her warm, naked body heats me. Even with the temperature lowered to fifty, I'm already starting to melt. An itchy tingle runs down my body as I begin to disappear.

"Shit," she says as she realizes what's happening. "We can't have that."

She disappears from my line of sight, then reappears with the hat in her hands. As she places it on my head again, a wave of relief rushes through me.

"At least I can see your cock now," she says with a giggle.

She nibbles her lower lip and drops to her knees in front of me. Warmth and pleasure engulf me, but I want to see it. I force the change back into a human, with her mouth still wrapped around my cock. When she sees the change, her eyes widen, but not just because I transformed into a human in front of her.

My large carrot cock still rests in her hand.

She throws herself backward and hits the back of her head on the island. I reach out to cushion her fall, but she bats me away with her hands. My greatest fear has become a reality. My cock disgusts her.

"Jesus fucking Christ!" she squeals. "What is that?"

"A carrot," I whisper.

"I know it's a fucking carrot, Frisky, but why . . ." She shakes her head. "Why is it still attached to your human form?"

"I don't know. It just is." I cover my crotch with my hands. "This is why I didn't want to show you."

She rubs the back of her head. "You misunderstand. This is nothing to be embarrassed about. You think I care that you have a carrot for a cock? I fuck vegetables more than I fuck real dicks."

"Real dicks?"

"You know what I mean. I'm not saying your dick isn't real. It's just . . . different." Her curious eyes rise to mine. "And it works?"

"To the best of my knowledge. But—"

"But nothing! You have my fucking dream dick attached to you! It's like I created my perfect man. Strong, sexy, chiseled, but with a carrot cock."

"Snow princess," I whisper, "I'm worried that fucking you will change everything."

"Of course it will change everything. I can't be the same person after I get fucked by the snowman I built."

She drags me back toward the bedroom with the strength of an army, and I'm powerless to stop her. When she reaches the bed, she heaves me onto the mattress with a feral glint in her eyes.

Oh god, it's happening.

I'll finally be able to experience my snow princess. Instead of sitting idle while her body works with mine, I can explore her body with my hands. I can push myself into her and fuck her the way she deserves to be fucked.

She straddles my lap, her hand rubbing along the length of my dick. Looking down as she touches me is a luxury I didn't experience as a snowman, and I take full advantage of it now. She puts my carrot cock inside her, and her warmth engulfs me. Her tightness squeezes me. And she was right. Nothing will be the same now.

"Fuck," I growl.

I grip her hips to keep her from moving on my lap. I can hardly handle being inside her. The anticipation coupled with her wet warmth is better than I expected, and I worry I'll come before I can please her.

"You feel so good." I suck air through my teeth as she pulses around me. "Too good."

I pull her off my cock and I come. Embarrassment flushes my face and chest as I hold her above my dick, spilling my pleasure onto my lap.

"Jesus Christ, Frisky! Is that . . . peppermint?" Her eyes narrow for a moment. "That's what was on my sheet that morning! You dirty fucking snowman," she says with a laugh.

I appreciate her not shaming me for my premature excitement.

She crawls down my body and wraps her mouth around my dick. Her tongue swirls over the tip and down my shaft, then travels over my abdomen as she cleans every trace of come from my skin.

"Yep, it's peppermint," she says as she licks her lips. "You never have to worry about me spitting."

She looks so beautifully dirty, and I can't wait to fill her with more of it. I pull her up to me and kiss her. I want to be happy in this moment. I should be. But a question nags at my mind.

What happens when the snow melts?

CHAPTER SEVEN

Holly

$\mathcal{E}$ven wrapped in his arms, my skin remains eternally pebbled, but Frisky can't handle normal temperatures. Even with my thermostat set at fifty degrees, his body lets off so much warmth. I feel like I'm lying beside a furnace.

My gaze keeps returning to his massive cock as it rests against his lower belly. My favorite shape. My preferred vegetable to fuck myself with. I only wish I could have experienced more of it. But I'll wait for him. I'm not at all disappointed. If anything, I'm flattered he couldn't control himself when he was inside me. The moment he's hard again, I'll ride him into next winter.

I lean into him and kiss him, and memories of licking his coal mouth flood my mind. His full lips are much more kissable now. They spread on mine, and his tongue pries into my mouth. I whimper against him. Much like his cock, his body, and everything else about him, this kiss feels like it was made just for me.

"Would you play with anyone else?" I ask.

"Never, snow princess. I'm yours and yours alone to use."

God, what words. How lucky am I to get the custom man of my dreams who's obsessed with my pleasure? It's a goddamn Christmas miracle.

"Be right back," he whispers, giving me a kiss as he slides out of bed. A few moments later, he returns with another carrot in his hand.

"What are you planning to do with that?" I ask as I sit up on my elbows.

"I'd rather show you," he says.

"Please do."

He smirks and pulls me to the edge of the bed by my thighs, then he turns me onto my stomach. I watch over my shoulder as he brings the carrot to his mouth and sucks on it before raising my hips. I have no idea what he plans to do, but I'm here for it.

He runs the carrot through my wet slit before he sticks the thin tip against my ass. Now I know what he wants to do, and I'm still here for it.

He pushes it inside me, stretching me so gently as he eases it in. I gasp as he pulls it back and pushes it inside again. The texture and natural ridges bump along sensitive nerves, filling me with pleasure. He rests his cock against my slit as he hardens. I bite my lip as he draws his hips back and pushes his tip inside me. I scream out, made so full by both vegetables.

"Frisky," I pant.

"Does that feel good, my snow princess? Do you like having two carrot cocks inside you?"

"I love it."

He stops moving the carrot in my ass as he increases the

tempo in my pussy. His hips pound harder and faster. Sweat drips down his body from the warmth in the house and the fire between my legs.

"Put me on my back," I moan.

Without removing anything from my body, he lifts me and turns me over. I raise my hips and change the angle as he pumps into me again, the carrot still filling my ass. I grip the sheets as he fucks me. I'm so full. I've died and gone to heaven, every fantasy fulfilled, including fantasies I didn't know I had.

Frisky leans down and takes my nipple into his mouth, sucking and licking until I see stars. His hand drops between us and rubs my clit. He really wants to draw one more out of me, and I'm more than happy to let him. It's incredibly easy for him to throw me over the edge with the perfect swirl of his fingers over my clit.

I come, and he grunts as I squeeze around him.

"Fuck, being inside you when you come is incredible, but witnessing you like this is indescribable. The way you writhe and bend from pleasure. The way your lips spread as you scream out. It brings me so fucking close. I want to fill you with my come. I want to see it dripping out of you. My naughty little snow princes."

"Give me your come," I moan. "Please fill me, Frisky."

As a rabid groan escapes his lips, he does just that. Warmth jets inside me, pulsing with each beat of his heart. And it just keeps coming. I feel myself filling, then the warmth drips down my ass when I can't hold any more. His groans finally wane, and I know he's emptied himself completely inside me.

His hands hook behind my knees as he lifts my legs and spreads me. "Show me," he commands.

As he pulls out of me, peppermint-scented air rushes toward me. "Let me taste it," I say.

He leans down, laps up some of the come, spreads my lips with one hand, and spits the come onto my tongue. I revel in the warm mixture of peppermint and my arousal.

His fingers return to my warmth, and he pushes his come deep inside me. He lowers his mouth to me again, laps up more come, and spits it on my pussy before fingering me some more.

Now I have an idea of my own. I sit up on my elbows, and he raises his eyes to mine. "I need a shower. And I want you to join me."

CHAPTER EIGHT

Frisky

She drags me to the bathroom and closes the door, then she twists a knob and water flows from a spout. As she turns toward me, her gaze rises to my hat.

"What do you think will happen if we take your hat off now?"

I smirk. "Your pussy is magical, snow princess, but I don't think it holds *that* kind of magic. Let's not turn me into a giant snowman in this little bathroom."

"Fair," she says as she pulls the shower curtain aside and climbs over the lip of the tub.

Steam wafts to the ceiling, and sweat collects on my brow. Unable to breathe in this warm space, I open the door and let the cool air race back into the bathroom.

"Aren't you coming in?" she says.

I look at her sweet face peeking from the side of the curtain. She wants me to get in the shower with her, but I don't know if I can handle the heat. I'm already melting. But I'll do anything for her.

I grit my teeth and step into the hellish spray. Her naked body is a nice consolation prize for the third-degree burns, so I tolerate it for as long as I can. Which doesn't turn out to be very long. I reach behind her and turn the shower to a cooler temperature.

Doubt creeps into my mind. She needs warmth, even if she likes the cold sometimes, but I need the cold *all* the time, even when I'm in my human form. How can this work?

When the water runs colder, goosebumps pebble her smooth skin. Her teeth begin to chatter, and her hands rub her arms. My job is to bring her pleasure, not make her miserable. I need to do something to make her feel good again. And fast.

I grip the showerhead and lift it from its holder, then I bring it between her legs. I turn the water all the way to cold, and she whimpers, crashing back against the wall as she tries to get away from the stream.

"Don't you like the cold?" I whisper against her mouth as I kiss her.

"I love the cold, but sometimes a little warmth is nice as well."

I listen to her needs and turn the temperature up again. Now that the stream isn't blazing against my skin, maybe I can tolerate this heat. Her whimpers turn into a soft moan, and I know I've made the right decision. Her hips move against the concentrated spray of water, and more soft sounds ease from her mouth. I play with the temperature, making the water cold again, then warm, then hot, and finally cold again. Her nails sink into my shoulders with each change.

"Do you like that, snow princess?"

"I don't think I can physically come again, Frisky," she pants.

"You can always come once more for me," I say, leaning into her and putting pressure on the showerhead. "You'll have to get used to coming around me. I live to please you. I exist to get you off."

"You're my snowman. The dirty fucking snowman I made," she says through a moan. "How is this possible?"

Her head drops back and her muscles tighten as the pleasure builds inside her, and each shock of ecstasy goes straight to my groin. I know when she's getting close. I feel it in my body.

Her thighs begin to quiver, and her grip tightens on my arms. "I'm coming!" she screams.

I ease her through the orgasm, holding her up as her muscles contract and relax. When she's ridden the last wave, I replace the showerhead and begin washing her hair and body. Her eyes rise to mine, and she puts soap in her hands. She rubs them together to lather them up, then she begins to bathe me. The intimacy of this act is almost as intense as the sex. It's such a human thing to do. So normal.

And I love it.

Can I ever go back to being a snowman after experiencing this with her? I can't imagine spending my days alone, far away from the woman I adore. If I'm being honest, the woman I love.

But I'll do whatever makes her happy. If that means I have to return to the snow, then so be it. I'll love her from afar, even as I melt.

We get out of the shower, and I nearly sweat to death as I wait for her to dress. As she towels her hair, I go to the front door, whip it open, and bathe my skin in the frigid air. I don't know how I'll make this temperature difference work, but I'll figure it out. I have to.

My snow princess clutches her robe around her and steps into the doorway. "Why are you outside?"

"I got a little warm in there. I don't know why the temperature affects me so much."

Her eyes scan my head. "Maybe it's the hat?"

"The hat isn't making me this warm. Besides, if I take it off, I'll be a snowman again."

"So? Try it."

"No thanks."

"For me?" she says with a pout of her lip.

Oh yeah, I'll do anything for her if she asks like that.

I grip the hat and clench my eyes shut as I lift the cap from my head. I wait. And wait. But I don't turn into a snowman. In fact, my bare feet start to feel cold, which is a terrible feeling. I run toward Holly and pick her up.

"I'm cold!" I shout before I kiss her. "And I'm human!"

"You're human," she says. She smiles at me, but a hint of sadness lingers in her eyes. Her distress lances my heart with a physical ache. I never wanted to disappoint her.

"I'll find a way to give you the cold again, snow princess. I promise."

EPILOGUE

ONE YEAR LATER

Holly

*H*eavy snow falls as I stare out the window. Big, fluffy flakes drift from the sky and join the growing blanket covering my yard. We've already gotten nearly a foot, and we're due for more overnight.

"Snow princess," he says.

His erection presses against my lower back, and I can't help but wonder if he remembers our time in the snow last year. How we began.

Our time together since last winter has been interesting. He's had to learn things that I was happy to teach him, and there were so many new experiences for both of us. I even gave him a new name—Dominick—because it was too awkward to call him Frisky in public.

One thing he never had to learn was how to please me. He's incredible at that, and it hasn't stopped being his sole mission in life. Being with him has changed me as a person.

A smile spreads on his face. "Let's go outside."

My eyes light up as we slide our feet into our boots. We dress in warm jackets, then we head out into the wintry world. Frisky looks so at home in this early snowfall, and it's always been my favorite event of the year. I drop to my knees in the yard and lie back on a blanket of white. An icy chill embraces my body.

Frisky tosses my hat to me, and I shove it on my head. He swirls his old beanie around his extended finger and smirks. "Shall we try?" he asks.

Oh god, yes please.

"Sure," I say. "But no matter what, I love you for you."

This isn't just an empty platitude. I'll love him even if he can no longer become a snowman.

He slips the hat onto his head and we wait. He closes his eyes and wiggles his feet. I close mine to blink, and when I open them again, a snowman stands before me, complete with his monster carrot cock.

My mouth waters for him as I sit up on my knees. I've never wanted anything more. Frisky in human form is amazing, but there's something special about straddling a big snowball body. Something about selfishly fucking myself with an inanimate object. But Frisky isn't inanimate, and that's what makes this even better. He'll feel everything and yearn to touch me when he can't. Like when he had me tied up, he'll get to be helpless this time.

I have been so lucky to have my kink come to life like this, to be absolutely spoiled by orgasms, and yet I still yearn to fuck my snowman. Frisky found a way to make it happen.

I lower my sweatpants and back up to his cold body. As the icy carrot presses against my warmth, I smile. "Merry Christmas, Frisky."

CONNECT WITH LAUREN

Check out LaurenBiel.com to sign up for the newsletter and get VIP (free and first) access to Lauren's spicy novellas and other bonus content!

Join the group on Facebook to connect with other fans and to discuss the books with the author. Visit http://www.face book.com/groups/laurenbieltraumances for more!

Lauren is now on Patreon! Get access to even more content and sneak peeks at upcoming novels. Check it out at www. patreon.com/LaurenBielAuthor to learn more!

ACKNOWLEDGMENTS

Thank you to my readers for bugging me about wanting a Lauren Biel Christmas story. Are you surprised this is how it ended up?

To my VIP gals (Lori, Kimberly, Jessie, Nikita, Lexi, Grace), I know you're excited about this story! My love for you all is endless!

A big, huge thank you to my husband, who insisted that Frisky maintained his giant carrot cock when he changed into his human form. (The amount of times I've said the words "carrot cock" in the last week should be illegal)

Thank you to my editor, Brooke, for always encouraging my weirdness!

Thank you to my valued Patrons! Your contribution helped make this book happen!

Lori (Special love your way, friend!), Michelle M, Tabitha F, Jessie S, Lindsey S, Erika M, Laura T, Kayla W, Jennifer S, Nicole M, Eugenia M, Nineette W, Kimberly B, Jessica C, BoneDaddyAshe, Diana W, Ashley T, Kimberly S, Sammie Rae, Sarah, Kay S, Allison B, Andrea J, Bethany R, Chelle, Gabby S, Hollie P, Jennifer H, Jessica G, Juli D, Samantha R, Sara S, XynideSuicide, @bethbetweenthepages, Sharee S,

Samantha W, Lourdes G, Kelli T, Kayla M, Victoria R, Shelby F, Lauren P, Mackenzie H, Tiannah B, Wombles, Kristiana B, Vero A, Amanda Kay A.

ALSO BY LAUREN BIEL

To view Lauren Biel's complete list of books, visit: https://laurenbiel.com/laurenbielbooks/

ABOUT THE AUTHOR

Lauren Biel is the author of many dark romance books with several more titles in the works. When she's not working, she's writing. When she's not writing, she's spending time with her husband, her friends, or her pets. You might also find her on a horseback trail ride or sitting beside a waterfall in Upstate New York. When reading her work, expect the unexpected. To be the first to know about her upcoming titles, please visit www.LaurenBiel.com.